D0561332

It's Not Easy Being a Bunny

by Marilyn Sadler

illustrated by
Roger Bollen

BEGINNER BOOKS   A Division of Random House, Inc.

Library of Congress Cataloging in Publication Data:
Bollen, Marilyn Sadler. It's not easy being a bunny. SUMMARY: Unhappy being a bunny, P. J. Funnybunny tries living with bears, birds, beavers, pigs, moose, possums, and skunks. [1. Rabbits—Fiction. 2. Animals—Fiction] I. Bollen, Roger, ill. II. Title. PZ7.B635913It 1983 [E] 83-2680 ISBN: 0-394-86102-7 (trade); 0-394-96102-1 (lib. bdg.)

Manufactured in the United States of America   4 5 6 7   I J K

P. J. Funnybunny was very sad.

He did not like being a bunny.

His mother made him eat
cooked carrots every day.

He had far too many
brothers and sisters.

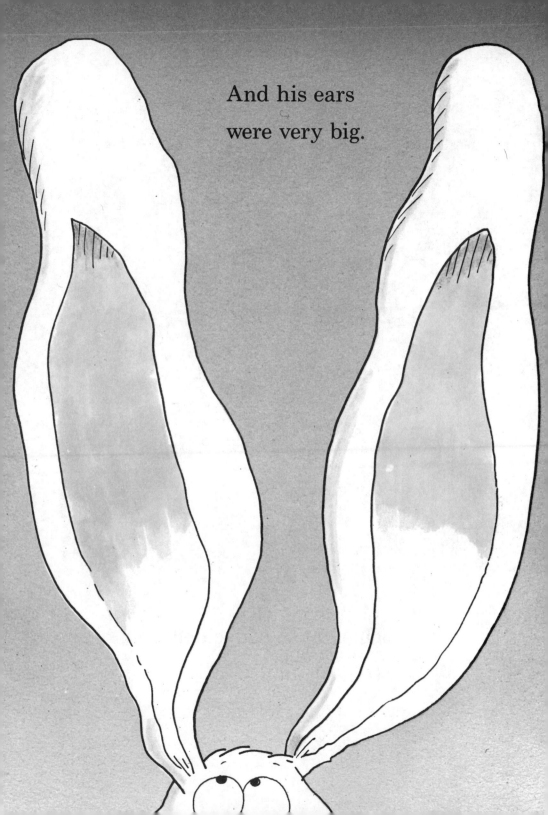

And his ears
were very big.

One day P. J. decided
to leave home.

"I don't want to be
a bunny anymore,"
said P. J.

"I want to be a...

...BEAR!"

And P. J. went to live
with the bears.

But when the bears
went to sleep
for the winter,
P. J. could not sleep
at all.
Living with the bears
was not very exciting.

So P. J. said,

"I don't want to be a bear.

I want to be a...

...BIRD!"

And P. J. went to live
with the birds.

P. J. liked being a bird—
until he tried to fly.

So P. J. said,
"I don't want to be a bear
OR a bird.
I want to be a...

And P. J. went to live
with the beavers.

The beavers liked to work
very hard.
P. J. did not like to work
at all.

So P. J. said,
"I don't want to be a bear
or a bird
OR a beaver.

I want to be a...

And P. J. went to live
with the pigs.

But the only thing
the pigs liked to do
was sit in the mud.

So P. J. said,

"I don't want to be a bear

or a bird

or a beaver

OR a pig.

I want to be a...

...MOOSE!"

And P. J. went to live
with the moose.

But P. J. could not make
good moose calls.

So P. J. said,
"I don't want to be a bear
or a bird
or a beaver
or a pig
OR a moose.

I want to be a...

...POSSUM!"

And P. J. went to live
with the possums.

The possums liked to hang
upside down.
But hanging upside down
gave P. J. a headache.

So P. J. said,

"I don't want to be a bear

or a bird

or a beaver

or a pig

or a moose

OR a possum.

I want to be a...

...SKUNK!"

And P. J. went to live
with the skunks.

It did not take P. J. very long
to find out that he did not like
living with the skunks.

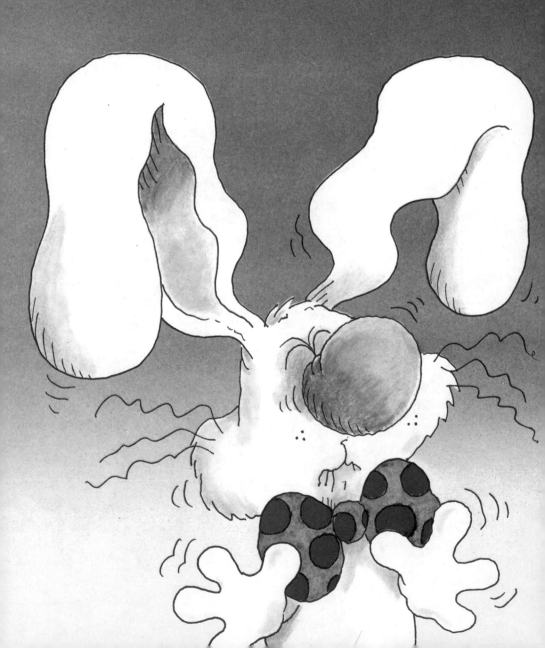

So P. J. said,

"I don't want to be a bear

or a bird

or a beaver

or a pig

or a moose

or a possum

OR, most of all, a skunk.

What I REALLY want to be is a...

So P. J. hurried home.
The Funnybunnies were very happy
to see him.
P. J. was very happy
to see them.

That night P. J. ate
all of his cooked carrots...

...and played with every one
of his brothers and sisters.

He was so happy
to be a bunny again
that he did not care
that his ears were very big.
"At least everyone can see
that I am a bunny," P. J. said,
"and not a...

...bear

or a bird

or a beaver

or a pig

or a moose

or a possum

or a skunk."